THE WAITING ROOM

Two Plays in One

ADEOLA OYEKOLA

The Waiting Room
All Rights Reserved.
Copyright 2020 by Adeola Oyekola
v3.0

This is a work of fiction. The events and characters described herein are imaginary and are not intended to refer to specific places or living persons. The opinions expressed in this manuscript are solely the opinions of the author and do not represent the opinions or thoughts of the publisher. The author has represented and warranted full ownership and/or legal right to publish all the materials in this book.

This book may not be reproduced, transmitted, or stored in whole or in part by any means, including graphic, electronic, or mechanical without the express written consent of the publisher except incase of brief quotations embodied in critical articles and reviews.

First Printing, 2018

http://www.olabooksinternationalselfpub.com

ISBN-13: 978-1-7353-6718-7

Printed in the United States of America

CONTENTS

THE WAITING ROOM

CAST

Narrator 1: An elderly male character who narrates the story to the audience

Narrator 2: An elderly female character who co-narrates the story to the audience

Haggai: A beautiful young maid

Sarah: A female voice in the background

Baby: Haggai's baby

Dance Troupe: Performing arts group

Ruth: An unhappy middle-aged woman waiting on God for a child

Gideon: A materialistic man who impatiently ruined his marriage

Mama: An inconsiderate mother-in-law

Ben: A man who influences his friend's decisions

Angela: A gossip

Pat: Gideon's second wife

This Play is written to show cultural diversity. You may explore any culture of your choice, as directed by the director.

SCENE ONE

(Two people are walking and having a conversation. They stop walking as they approach the middle of the stage.)

NARRATOR 1:

My sister, I was meditating the other day about families in the Bible and I concluded that there is no perfect family in the Bible.

NARRATOR 2:

Really?

NARRATOR 1:

I can give you many examples: (Counting his fingers) Adam and Eve, Noah's family, Abraham's family, Lot's family, Isaac's family, Jacob's family, King Saul's family, David's family, Solomon's family, Jesus' family and so on.

NARRATOR 2:

Stop right there! Blasphemer! What do you mean counting all those families, including Jesus' family?

NARRATOR 1:

I will explain it to you…

NARRATOR 2:

You should.

NARRATOR 1:

Adam and Eve…

NARRATOR 2:

I know about Adam and Eve. Tell me about Jesus' family.

NARRATOR 1:

Oh, very simple. Jesus' parents did not realize that he was still in Jerusalem after they had left. They traveled an entire day's journey before they realized he was not with them. They also had to look for him for three days before they found him.

NARRATOR 2:

Parental negligence.

NARRATOR 1:

You're right.

NARRATOR 2:

But he chose to stay behind to do "His Father's work."

NARRATOR 1:

Parents need to be vigilant. That is still negligence.

NARRATOR 2:

You're right. Tell me about Abraham, the father of all nations and the righteous one before God. What do you have against him?

NARRATOR 1:

Abraham was not only righteous before God, but he was also a man of faith. God blessed him and because of him, he also blessed the generations after him, including our generation. God promised to give him and his wife a child even in their old age, but he was not ready to wait on God. He tried to help God out by getting his maid pregnant…

NARRATOR 2:
I knew you would say that. If you read your Bible more carefully, you would know that it was Sarah, his wife, who asked him to do it.

NARRATOR 1:
Hmm… his wife. But we are talking about a family here. Decision making is very important. They both agreed to do it and it was done. They didn't pray over it, neither did they think about it. Rather, out of their desperation to have a child, they agreed. I believe Hagar was an exquisite maid.

(Hagar walks in, beautifully dressed, smiling and holding a pitcher as if she is about to fetch water. She stops in front of the narrators and curtsies in greeting. They wave at her and she walks away)

NARRATOR 2:
Dutiful, too.

NARRATOR 1:
As you can see…, Father Abraham could not resist her. The temptation was too much: the beauty, the hard work, and the recommendation from his wife. I am sure Sarah knew her husband's taste in women too.

NARRATOR 2:
She would not have chosen the worst of their maids; she would have chosen the best for her husband.

NARRATOR 1:

Now you are thinking like I am. Everything was there physically to entice Abraham to Hagar. (Looking narrator 2 straight in the eye.)

Never blame your spouse for a joint decision. If you agree to it then it's your fault too.

NARRATOR 2:

Hmm … two are better than one. We should weigh all the sides of a decision before concluding.

NARRATOR 1:

Most importantly, pray over it and wait for an answer from God before you go ahead with your decision.

NARRATOR 2:

Yes, (nodding) but you need to finish the story.

NARRATOR 1:

Yes, Hagar had the baby and became proud.

(Hagar walks in again, carrying her baby. Sarah calls Hagar in the background, but she refuses to answer, turning to the audience she says…)

HAGAR:

Why is the barren woman calling me? Do you think I am still your maid? We share the same man and I have a child. You do not. You will probably die barren, anyway. (She walks away.)

NARRATOR 2:
What insolence!

NARRATOR 1:
That was why Sarah sent her away with her son; she couldn't live with the happy family.

NARRATOR 2:
Hmm… interesting. Introducing Hagar into their family wasn't a pleasant situation.

NARRATOR 1:
No, it wasn't. Find out about Hagar's son, Ishmael, in your private time. Then you can draw your conclusions about the story.

NARRATOR 2:
I will, it is an interesting, historical story.

NARRATOR 1:
Now that you're thinking like I am, can you relate this story to a modern-day story?

NARRATOR 2:
(Touching her forehead, thinking.)
Yes! Yes! Yes! This story happened in the western part of Nigeria. It is very much like the story of Abraham and Sarah.

(We hear drum beats and both dance off stage.)

(BLACKOUT)

Scene Two

(A Yoruba traditional marriage is going on. People are singing and dancing and beating the drums. The couple are the center of attraction and people hail them as they vigorously dance to the music.)

Songs
Oni lojo ayo re, lojo ayo re, lojo ayo re/2x
Iyawo abibeji b'Oluwa bafe/2x
Eje ojo ooo eje ojo
Iyawo ojo latana, eje ojo

(After some rounds of the songs, the moderator calls on the parents of the groom to pray for the couple. After the prayers, the troupe dance off the stage. The couple first, then the choreography troupe.)

(BLACKOUT)

SCENE THREE

(A love seat, some paintings on the wall, beautiful flowers, and a center table are used to represent a lavishly furnished living room.)

RUTH:
(Walks in, dressed in Western attire, looking incredibly sad. She looks at the audience and begins a prologue.)
That was my wedding. Very colorful, it was the talk of the town for several months afterwards. It has been five years now and I have no child to show for it. (Sniffs back tears) My in-laws have been pressuring me to give them children, especially my mother-in-law and sisters-in-law. I have prayed and fasted; men of God have prophesied and laid hands on my stomach; and I have gone through many deliverance sessions, all to no avail. All I hear in my spirit is "patience." I hear "patience" each time I pray or think about it, but for how long? I have no answer (sits down dejectedly.) Something must happen soon because I don't think I have enough room for the patience God is asking for. (Gideon walks in.)

GIDEON:
You do, my dear wife (sitting beside her.) Job said, "All the days of my appointed time will I wait until my change cometh." We have no choice but to wait on God to fulfill our heart's desires.

RUTH:
(smiles) Thank you, darling. You are such a wonderful husband and I love you so much.

(we hear Mama off-stage talking with a loud voice.)

MAMA:

Ekule nbi o. Talo wanle oo?

RUTH:

(Her sweet countenance changes to that of fear.)

That's Mama!

GIDEON:

Yes.

MAMA:

(Comes on-stage dressed in traditional attire.)

Ekule oo!

RUTH:

(Kneels in greeting)

Welcome, Mama.

MAMA:

(Ignores her and sits down.)

RUTH:

Welcome, Mama.

MAMA:

I am not deaf like you. I heard you the first time but didn't answer you.

GIDEON:

Welcome, Mama. (Prostrating himself)

MAMA:

(Smiling) *Okare oko mi.* How are you? How is work? I hope you are fine.

GIDEON:

I am fine. But why didn't you answer Ruth when she greeted you? She is still on her knees.

MAMA:

Didn't she hear me when I first greeted her? After all, she was sitting here with you and she should have rushed to the door to give me a warm welcome. It's not as if she was doing anything important. She's not nursing a baby, or cooking for the children-What could be more important than me?

RUTH:

But Mama, I greeted you as soon as you walked into the house.

MAMA:

Shut up!

GIDEON:

Mamaaa! Please leave us alone. God will give us children in his own time. I have told you several times to stop molesting my wife because we do not have children. It's not her fault; we are together in this.

MAMA:

It is her fault! Let her confess to you what she did before she met you. She cannot have children; she is barren.

RUTH:

Ha! Mama! (Bursts into tears and runs off-stage with Gideon following and calling her name.)

MAMA:

The truth must be told. Those are crocodile tears; they do not move me. As for you, Gideon, you will come back to meet me here. I know you are the loyal son of your father. *Mi bimo ale ri, Olorun maje!*

(BLACKOUT)

SCENE FOUR

(A couch convertible bed is used to represent lavishly furnished bedroom. Ruth is lying on her bed reading a Bible when her phone rings.)

RUTH:

Hello…! Hello darling…! How was your flight…? I haven't slept since you left because I've been missing you, and waiting for you to call… Now that I have heard your voice, I can sleep… Alright darling, be sure to call me first thing in the morning… Take care of yourself… Talk to you later… Love you too.

(Sighs. Looking at the phone) Good to hear your voice. I will be without my husband for six months. God, I need your help. (Goes to sleep. Light fades.)

(BLACKOUT

SCENE FIVE

(The narrators come back on-stage dancing to the traditional drum as the light comes on.)

NARRATOR 1:
You are still an excellent dancer.

NARRATOR 2:
You too.

NARRATOR 1:
But next time, I will clearly win the dance.

NARRATOR 2:
Let's wait till then.

NARRATOR 1:
We shall see. That aside, you need to finish your story.

NARRATOR 2:
Yes, Gideon changed his mind about staying in America for six months. He saw America as a land of opportunities and his friend promised to help him with his papers, so he stayed longer.

NARRATOR 1:
What about his wife? What about having children?

(Both walking off-stage)

NARRATOR 2:

(sarcastically)

Remember, they were going to wait on the Lord until the appointed time.

13

NARRATOR 1:

Are you serious?

(BLACKOUT)

SCENE SIX

(As the narrators walk off the stage on one side, Gideon walks in from another entrance talking on the phone, obviously to his wife.)

GIDEON:
Please try to understand me… I know… but this will be life chang-ing for us… I want children as much as you do. Opportunities come but once. Let's grab it, darling… My friend will help me with the papers… It's easy… I will give you the details… Yes, I say so… Trust me, everything will be fine. Love you too… Talk to you later.

(Off the phone) Women and their problems! I need to call Mama.

(He dials, and we hear mama's voice offstage.)

MAMA:
Oko miii, se alaafia lo wa?

GIDEON:
Beeni maami. How are you and everyone at home?

MAMA:
We are fine. I am so happy to hear your voice.

GIDEON:
I'm glad to hear from you.

MAMA:
Although I miss you, I like your decision to stay longer, especially because it involves a woman.

GIDEON:

It involves a woman on paper. I told you I am only married to her on paper–nothing more. She will help me secure a legal stay in America.

MAMA:

We are saying the same thing. You married her on paper; it means both of you are married and she can bear you children.

GIDEON:

Mama, please listen to me. This is an arranged marriage. After I get what I want from her, we will divorce.

MAMA:

Before you divorce, please ensure that you get her pregnant.

GIDEON:

Mama, what you are suggesting is not biblical.

MAMA:

Is it biblical to lie to the government about your marital status? Huh? Is it biblical to have two wives? Is it biblical to want to use an illegal means to get what you want? I need an answer from you.

GIDEON:

You need to understand that this is a once-in-a-lifetime opportunity.

MAMA:

I understand, and that is why I am saying you should use your once-in-a-lifetime opportunity to have a child. When next I call you, I want to hear that your new wife is pregnant. *O daaro.*

GIDEON:

Goodnight, Maami.

(Hangs up. Sighs bows down his head dejectedly. His friend walks in.)

BEN:

Hey, man! What's up?

GIDEON:

Hey. (Face bump)

BEN:

How's everything going?

GIDEON:

Fine.

BEN:

Fine? Pat wasn't fine a couple of minutes ago.

GIDEON:

What's wrong with her?

BEN:

That girl is into you. She loves you.

GIDEON:

That is not our agreement. She helped me. I am married, for God's sake. I can't do what she wants.

BEN:

But you married her.

GIDEON:

But it's only on paper. I mean, I don't understand you guys. You say one thing today and another tomorrow.

BEN:

For how long do you want to run away from women? I am not even suggesting to you to go after other women. I am talking to you about your wife. America knows you to have one wife — your American wife. And you don't want a divorce before you get what you want from her, do you?

GIDEON:

No, I don't. I will think about it.

BEN:

Don't think about it, do something about it. This might be your only chance to have a child.

GIDEON:

(sighs) My mother said the same thing.

BEN:

She did? Mothers are always right (patting him on the back.) You are on the right path; trust your buddy. You are on the right path. (Leads him off-stage)

(BLACKOUT)

Scene Seven

(Narrators back on stage)

NARRATOR 2:
Gideon's second wife got pregnant like his mom, and friend advised. She had a set of twins. But his first wife remained faithful to him. God made a way for her to visit her husband. He hurriedly rented an apartment and furnished it so that his wife wouldn't find out he has another woman.

NARRATOR 1:
Did Ruth find out?

NARRATOR 2:
She did.

(As they leave the stage, Ruth walks in, singing.)

(BLACKOUT)

Scene Eight

RUTH:

(After singing and dancing) God, I thank you for the blessing of the fruit of the womb. I am pregnant after all these years. I endured mockery here and there. Some people said I was barren; some said I had lost my womb to a series of abortions, but I am grateful today that I am pregnant, not with one child but two. God is great! (Doorbell rings) Yes, come in.

ANGELA:
Good afternoon, Sister Ruth.

RUTH:
Good afternoon, Sister Angela. You finally made it to my home, I am so happy to see you.

ANGELA:
Same here.

RUTH:
Please, have a seat while I get you something to eat.

ANGELA:
Please, don't worry about giving me something to eat; I am fine. I came here to ask you a question.

RUTH:
I am all ears.

ANGELA:

Do you know Sister Pat?

RUTH:

Sister Pat? I don't know anyone by that name. You know I am new in this area; I hardly know anybody.

ANGELA:

I said so. I said you don't know her. I told Sister Racheal you wouldn't know.

RUTH:

What about the sister?

ANGELA:

She is Brother Gideon's wife.

RUTH:

(Smiles) Wife? No, I am Gideon's wife. You probably got it mixed up.

ANGELA:

You are the one getting it mixed up. You need to confront him with the information. He cannot deny it. He married Sister Pat, and she has two children by him.

RUTH:

Angela, get out of my home right now. I don't need your friendship.

ANGELA:

I will leave but you will eventually look for me because, out of all the people who know the truth, I am the only one who shed some light on your darkness (She leaves.)

RUTH:

Could this be true? Gideon married to another woman? Oh my God! (Holds her tummy) Oh, my baby! Oh, what a shame! What will I do ... ? Angela, wait; please wait ... (She runs after Angela.)

(BLACKOUT)

SCENE NINE

(Gideon sits in a chair dejectedly in their living room. Ruth is pacing up and down in tears.)

RUTH:

I was hoping you would deny it, but you didn't. Why did you do it?

GIDEON:

(Sober) I did it for love.

RUTH:

You love her?

GIDEON:

No, I mean, I love you. I was thinking about the beautiful life we could share as a family when I eventually got you here.

RUTH:

No, don't lie to me, you were thinking about raising a family here because you believed that I was barren. God has proved you wrong.

GIDEON:

I had always believed we would have children. Things got out of hand. I didn't plan on bringing a "Hagar" into our family.

RUTH:

What family are you talking about? I cannot stay married to you after this betrayal. I also heard that you produced fake divorce papers so you could get married again. You may consider those papers as originals. I am out of your life!

GIDEON:

You can't do this to me. After all, you encouraged me to stay here in America to achieve everything I could achieve.

RUTH:

What are you insinuating? That I advised you to get married again? We were living a good life in Nigeria. Money was not our problem. You could have come back home.

GIDEON:

When I was coming to America, I told you I sensed a reluctance in my spirit about going, but you said I should go, anyway. You said God would make the crooked paths straight. If we had taken time to ask the Lord about it, nothing like this would have happened.

RUTH:

Now I am to blame? Who wouldn't think going to America was an open door from God? Well, I am out of your life. Stay married to your wife. Good riddance to bad rubbish! (She leaves.)

GIDEON:

What have I done to myself? (Walks away sad)

(BLACKOUT)

Scene Ten

(Gideon walks in, followed by his wife, Pat.)

PAT:

Where do you think you are going? You cannot walk out on me. I demand an answer from you.

GIDEON:

And what is the question?

PAT:

Who is Ruth?

GIDEON:

She is my wife.

PAT:

Was your wife, you mean?

GIDEON:

Whatever you say.

PAT:

You mean you lied to me? You told me you divorced your wife!

GIDEON:

Now you know the truth.

PAT:

You played on my intelligence. You lied to me!

GIDEON:

You abridged the contract when you started asking me for the intimacy I did not bargain for. What did you want me to do?

PAT:

Are you saying it is my fault you did not divorce your wife, and you married me?

GIDEON:

We arranged my marriage to you. You asked to make it real.

PAT:

You wanted to use me and dump me. You wanted me to be the loser by using me to get your stay in America and then run back to your wife and leave me empty-handed.

GIDEON:

Including emotions was not a part of the deal. You started this total mess.

PAT:

You cheated me, now you are blaming me. If it is the last thing I do, I swear to God you will live to regret this. (Storms out and storms back in.)

It is over between us. Run back to your darling wife. I swear with my last breath, you will rot in jail!

GIDEON:

Empty threats! If you go to the police, I will expose you too. Don't you forget I have some of your secrets that can land you in jail.

PAT:

If that's how it works, I will not make a report, but you will pay with heavy sweat!

(BLACKOUT)

SCENE ELEVEN

(Narrators come back on stage.)

NARRATOR 2:

Both Ruth and Pat left Gideon.

NARRATOR 1:

I see! But with Abraham, he did not marry Hagar, and he got Hagar pregnant because his wife wanted it.

NARRATOR 2:

You are right. Ruth was not interested in becoming an American citizen but thought that if she had prayed over her husband's decision to go to America in the first place, she would have saved her marriage. To them, going to America sounded like the greatest thing that could have happened to them. She forgave her husband after he pleaded with her. She took him back. They had their babies, but the woman and the children from the other marriage were thorns in their flesh for the rest of their lives. Those were not empty threats.

NARRATOR 1:

Hmm. So, the lesson is, "Stay in the waiting room for God's manifestation." God can never be late.

NARRATOR 2:

No. Maybe Gideon should have waited for the right time to travel abroad with his wife. Maybe he should have gone back to Nigeria after six months. Maybe, maybe, just maybe, they would have had their own children without thorns in their flesh.

NARRATOR 1:
On second thought, did Ruth go back to Nigeria?

NARRATOR 2:
No. She came in with a student visa, got a work permit, and the company that hired her filed for her. Eventually she became a permanent resident.

NARRATOR 1:
How gracious can God be!

NARRATOR 2:
If only Gideon had waited, he would have received the same opportunity his wife got because they were writing the qualifying test every year. He would have passed too.

NARRATOR 1:
That leads me to my story, a story like that of Isaac's family.

NARRATOR 2:
It's getting dark. Why not tell me your story tomorrow?

NARRATOR 1:
Tomorrow, then. (Drums. They leave the stage.)

(BLACKOUT)

THE END

THE CHRISTMAS PRESENT

A One-Act Play

By

Adeola Oyekola

Cast

Dr. Thompson: A lonely man who works around the clock to relieve himself of his loneliness.

Mr. Greg: An old man who makes friends with his neighbors

Liz/Ms. Smith: A young Christian girl believing God for a better financial lifestyle

Cara: A young Christian girl frustrated about her financial status

Pastor: Leader of a church

Choir: A group of people singing a Christmas carol

Jesus Christ: A man in white flowing apparel

Small voice: A voice in the background

There are two more people buying from the yard sale.

Scene One

(A living room furnished with a love seat, a center table with a vase of flowers and some paintings on the wall. This scene represents Dr. Thompson's living room throughout the play. Dr. Thompson comes back from work looking tired. As he walks in, he tosses his car keys on the table and sits dejectedly.)

DR. THOMPSON:
I am so tired. What a busy day today was! (He looks at his wrist-watch) And to think I have another shift in the next three hours? I need a quick nap.

(He rests his head on the back of his chair and closes his eyes. He dreams. His dream happens somewhere beside or behind him, depending on how spacious the stage is. The dream: A man in white flowing apparel walks in. He pauses at the entrance and knocks on the door about three times. He stays there for a couple of minutes and leaves when there is no response. As this scene is going on, a solemn song is too: Holy, holy, holy, holy, holy, holy, holy, holy is the Lord/2x. Thompson wakes up with a start.)

This dream again? (A knock on his door) Who could that be? (Startled) The visitor in my dream? I don't have visitors except by appointment.

(Knock again. Opens the door. An old man walks in with a walking stick, a hat and a pot pipe in his mouth.)

Hello, sir! What can I do for you?

MR. GREG:

(Stretches out his hand for a handshake.)

Good evening. I am Mr. Greg, your neighbor.

DR. THOMPSON:

Good evening, Mr. Greg, I am …

MR. GREG:

Dr. Thompson. I know you very well. You drive past my house every day and never bother to say hi. You work around the clock and have no social life.

DR. THOMPSON:

To what do I owe this visit? (Getting irritated)

MR. GREG:

I have a yard sale coming up tomorrow evening and I stopped by to invite you.

DR. THOMPSON:

I must work tomorrow evening. I appreciate your invitation, but I cannot make it.

MR. GREG:

I wouldn't take your work time. It's about this time tomorrow — the same time you get your nap for the day. You have a beautiful house. (Steps in to inspect) So beautiful and clean and you don't live in it. How can you live in your own house for only two to three hours every day?

DR. THOMPSON:
Tomorrow evening? I'll be there. Thank you for your time.

MR. GREG:
I get it; forgive an old man's ramblings. I just get curious; that's what that is. See you tomorrow. (He leaves)

DR. THOMPSON:
Nosy old man. He has no life.

(He hears a small voice)

SMALL VOICE:
You have no life.

DR. THOMPSON:
(Emphatically)
I have a life! I save lives every day, help the needy and never stingy with my money. And I enjoy what I do for a living. Why would you say I have no life?

SMALL VOICE:
You have no life.

DR. THOMPSON:
It's a waste of time arguing with you.

(Looks at his wristwatch.)

I must go.

(He grabs his car keys and moves to leave as he hears the small voice again.)

SMALL VOICE:
You need a life.

(Dr. Thompson stops in his tracks, shakes his head angrily and moves on.)

(BLACKOUT)

Scene Two

(The yard sale. Two tables out to display some items. Mr. Greg stands by, attending to people as they come looking for what they can buy and making payments. Four people, including Dr. Thompson, come in. They each pick unique items.)

MS. SMITH:
(Picks a dress)
This looks good. I can wear this on Christmas Eve. How much, Mr. Greg?

MR. GREG:
I would appreciate anything you give.

(She gives him some money.)

Thank you!

MS. SMITH:
No, thank you. I was at the shopping mall the other day and couldn't pay for a beautiful dress I would have loved to wear for Christmas. Now, you are letting me pay what I want for this dress. I really appreciate it.

MR. GREG:
You are most welcome. Do you know that was a dress for my daughter many years ago? She never wore it.

MS. SMITH:

Sorry to hear that, Mr. Greg, but I love this dress.

MR. GREG:

Merry Christmas!

MS. SMITH:

Merry Christmas!

DR. THOMPSON:

(After she leaves)
Who was that lady?

MR. GREG:

You mean Ms. Smith? Don't tell me you don't know her. She lives next door to you.

DR. THOMPSON:

Are you kidding me?

MR. GREG:

You need some humor, don't you? That will help loosen up the serious look on your face.

DR. THOMPSON:

Mr. Greg, please spare me …

MR. GREG:

I know … forgive an old man. So, what are you picking up?

DR. THOMPSON:

I have looked around but couldn't find anything I could use.

MR. GREG:

I have some books right here. You find a good title for yourself.

(Thompson looks through and picks out a book, reading the title aloud.)

DR. THOMPSON:

"Your Life"

MR. GREG:

That's your choice? It's an excellent book. It will do you a lot of good.

DR. THOMPSON:

How much?

MR. GREG:

I will appreciate anything you give.

(Thompson gives him money)

I am sorry; I have no change.

DR. THOMPSON:

I don't need change. It's all yours.

MR. GREG:

This is too much (Breaks into tears.) You bless a lonely old man with this? God bless you.

DR. THOMPSON:

Amen. Buy yourself something good for Christmas.

MR. GREG:

Merry Christmas!

DR. THOMPSON:

Merry Christmas!

(BLACKOUT)

Scene Three

(A shabby living room with two chairs and a small wooden table. Liz is showing her new dress to her sister, Cara. Cara doesn't seem to be interested.)

LIZ:

Cara, look at this dress. Isn't it beautiful? I love it. God bless Mr. Greg for the yard sale.

CARA:

Why are you always excited about everything? What is beautiful about the dress?

LIZ:

It is beautiful, my idea of a Christmas dress. Come on, Cara, who will know I bought this from a yard sale after I wash and iron it.

CARA:

Liz, sit down and listen to me.

LIZ:

Okay. (She sits.)

CARA:

Have you ever sat down to think about when poverty will end in our lives? Look at you rejoicing over an old dress from Mr. Greg's yard sale. Only God knows how long that dress has been in his basement. It smells so old I don't want to believe you could touch it — not to mention wear this?

LIZ:

Cara, I always tell you that in everything we should give thanks. We don't have enough today, but we will have so much tomorrow. Trust me, I am wearing an old dress today, but if I remain faithful to God, I will wear new and expensive outfits tomorrow.

CARA:

Tomorrow?

LIZ:

Tomorrow could be tomorrow, or the future. But I know that I will not allow despair, anxiety, and frustration to take over my life. I will rejoice in the little I have and move on with my life, knowing that one day, someday, I will make it in life.

(A knock on the door. They exchange looks.)

CARA:

Are you expecting someone?

LIZ:

No.

CARA:

Who could that be? We never have visitors (Another knock) I'm scared.

LIZ:

Me too. (They huddle together.)

LIZ:

Come in, the door is open.

(Thompson walks in. Girls exchange looks again.)

DR. THOMPSON:

Good evening.

LIZ:

Good evening, sir.

DR. THOMPSON:

May I come in?

LIZ:

(Getting herself together)

Yes, please, come in. Excuse my manners.

DR. THOMPSON:

Thanks. My name is…

CARA:

Dr. Thompson, and you live next door.

DR. THOMPSON:

Oh… since I need no introduction, maybe you should introduce yourselves.

CARA:

My name is Cara, and this is my sister…

DR. THOMPSON:
Ms. Smith.

LIZ:
Last name, Smith — same as my sister — first name, Elizabeth. Liz for short.

DR. THOMPSON:
Nice to meet you.

LIZ and CARA:
Nice to meet you, sir.

(They shake hands.)

CARA:
To what do we owe this visit?

DR. THOMPSON:
I saw Liz earlier at Mr. Greg's yard sale and kind of felt like stopping by to say hello.

LIZ:
We are pleased to have you here. Please have a seat.

(Cara tries to wipe the chair clean to make it look more presentable.)

DR. THOMPSON:
I would have loved to, but I am in a rush. I came to give you something. I overheard what you told Mr. Greg about the dress you

couldn't afford to pay for. (Cara and Liz exchange looks) Believe me, I wasn't listening. I just overheard it and thought I could help pay for it if you wouldn't mind.

LIZ:
Thank you for the offer, but I now have a dress.

DR. THOMPSON
The dress from Mr. Greg. I know, and I saw you pay three dollars for it. How much was the dress you wanted at the shopping mall?

LIZ:
It was fifty dollars.

DR. THOMPSON:
(Gives her money.)
Here is two hundred. Buy two — one for you and one for your sister. You may keep the rest to buy something to cook for Christmas.

LIZ and CARA:
Thank you, sir!

DR. THOMPSON:
You're welcome. I'll take my leave now.

LIZ and CARA:
Thank you, sir. Thank you so much.

(After he leaves, the girls jump up, screaming for joy and struggling over who will keep the money.)

(BLACKOUT)

Scene Four

(Thompson at home reading the book, "Your Life." He stops and bursts out crying.)

DR. THOMPSON:
It's been five years. I thought it was over but now it's coming back so fresh, so fresh I am about to go insane!

(He throws a cup in anger.)

I need help. I really need help.

(Calms down)

What is life all about, anyway? It is meaningless, full of frustration and resentment. Can it be any better?

(A knock on the door.)

Mr. Greg again? I need a break!

(Another knock. He opens the door.)

LIZ:
(Comes in)
Good evening, Dr. Thompson. I hope I am not intruding?

DR. THOMPSON:
No, you're not. Good evening. Come in and have a seat.

LIZ:

Thank you, but I am in a hurry. I came to invite you to a Christmas carol service at my church tomorrow evening — Christmas Eve.

(Passes out a flyer)

I hope you can make it.

DR. THOMPSON:
I'll see what I can do.

LIZ:
Thank you, sir. See you tomorrow.

DR. THOMPSON:
Hopefully.

LIZ:
I believe you will make it.

DR. THOMPSON:
Will you be singing too?

LIZ:
Yes.

DR. THOMPSON:
I will be there.

LIZ:
Thank you, sir.

DR. THOMPSON:
You're welcome. (She leaves.) What a beautiful girl! She has a lovely smile too (Mr. Greg walks in.)

MR. GREG:
(Clears his throat)
You will need my permission before you can talk to her.

DR. THOMPSON:
(Startled)
Can anything I do miss your attention, Mr. Greg?

MR. GREG:
(Laughs)
I was just messing with you.

DR. THOMPSON:
You always do. That was nothing. She came to invite me to a carol service.

(He shows him the flyer.)

MR. GREG:
I got one too. I was wondering why you missed your evening shift.

DR. THOMPSON:
(Turns sober. Sighs.)
I called it off because I needed some time alone.

MR. GREG:
Interesting… If you don't mind, may I share your thoughts?

DR. THOMPSON:
I do mind. I don't share it. It's my life.

MR. GREG:
I am tired of keeping mine to myself; I want to share it. Would you mind listening or am I intruding?

DR. THOMPSON:
Have a seat, Mr. Greg. I'm all ears.

(They both sit.)

MR. GREG:
(Sits relaxed on the love seat and adjusts his hat and his pot pipe.)
It's a short, sad story. I had a beautiful wife and two lovely girls. I loved the younger, Tracy, more than the older, Adriana, and I would flaunt my love for Tracy in Adriana's face by buying Tracy beautiful accessories, dresses, shoes, you name it. Anything money could buy or that she asked for, I would buy. I always made excuses for Tracy each time she was wrong. I loved Adriana too, but I always made her pay for every wrong and bought her things after I had first satisfied Tracy. My wife called my attention to it several times, but I always made the excuse that Tracy was younger. Adriana should understand why Tracy gets something first.

(Stands and walks around the room, fighting back tears.)

It happened fifteen years ago today, the day before Christmas Eve. I had bought Tracy a beautiful red dress for Christmas. My wife nagged me until I went to the store to buy one for Adriana. My wife must have said something to Adriana about it because she went into my room when I was out picking a dress for her and she took the dress. She showed it to her sister and threatened to rip it in pieces. Tracy tried to retrieve it from her, but she ran out of the house and kept running because she was so jealous until she ran into a moving car, driving over the speed limit. I saw the car hit my daughter. She died.

DR. THOMPSON:
Oh, God!

MR. GREG:
Her mother never forgave me. She filed for divorce. She sold the house and took Tracy away with her. I have never heard from them since then.

DR. THOMPSON:
Sad story. Just like mine. Only, in my story, they all died.

MR. GREG:
Spill it out. We can handle this together.

DR. THOMPSON:
I had a boy and a girl. I loved the boy so much that I couldn't hide it. When he turned sixteen, I bought him a luxury car. My wife warned me, as always. She said the boy wasn't ready for a car. I still remember her choice of words clearly:

A LADY'S VOICE:
"Tom, I know Mark very well. He is too restless to handle a car. Let's wait another year or two."

DR. THOMPSON:
I said, "No, he asked for it." I could afford it, and he could drive. Why wait? He would learn some skills on the road. So, I bought it. My daughter Susan asked for a new dresser. I told her to give me some time, I had to buy her brother's car first because he was older. That was my usual saying. I bought the car. He was excited and wanted to drive around in his new car. Not sure of his driving skills, my wife hopped in beside him, thinking she could caution him if he started getting reckless. Susan wanted to be a part of it, so she went with them. That was the last I saw of my family. It was a deadly crash. None of them made it to the hospital.

(The two men hug and cry.)

MR. GREG:
(Finally breaking away.)
We both learned our lessons in a hard way, but we didn't have to. We could have learned from Isaac. The story of Jacob and Esau was good enough if we had paid close attention to it.

DR. THOMPSON:
But Jacob and Esau did not die.

MR. GREG:
That's right. I think God took our families away because He thought we did not deserve them. Or we gave the devil a chance to come in. I don't know.

DR. THOMPSON:

I think God took them away, and that is my anger against Him. He could have let them live and I would have corrected my ways.

MR. GREG:

(An abrupt laugh)

What would the world look like if God was partial?

DR. THOMPSON:

I guess there would be no one to run to, 'cos God would be human and not God anymore.

MR. GREG:

So, if God's intention is to make you a leader over his people, and he tests you with a family of four, you being the leader, and you favor one over the other, what are you doing?

DR. THOMPSON:

Creating enmity.

MR. GREG:

The war in the family will continue till eternity. You will settle disputes for the rest of your life. So, where is the place for your ministry, your daughters, or your sons?

DR. THOMPSON:

(Sighs heavily.)

I'll just say some mistakes are so fatal that there are no second chances.

MR. GREG:

I am with you on that one. God loves children so much he said in Matthew 18 verse 10 "See that you do not despise one of these little ones. For I tell you that, in heaven, their angels always see the face of my Father who is in heaven."

DR. THOMPSON:

I know He took them away from me, but He could have given me another chance.

MR. GREG:

Maybe He is giving you one, and you are running away from Him.

(They exchange looks for a minute)

I've repented, and I talk to Him every day. I know he will bring restoration to me somehow. You need to do the same. Let's meet at the carol service tomorrow.

(Pats his back and leaves)

(BLACKOUT)

Scene Five

(The choir is singing carols)
Long time ago in Bethlehem
So, the Holy Bible say
Mary's boy child, Jesus Christ
Was born on Christmas Day.

Hark now hear the angels sing
A king was born today
And man will live forevermore
Because of Christmas Day.

While shepherds watched their flock by night

They saw a bright new shining star
They heard a choir sing
The music seemed to come from afar

Hark, now hear the angels sing,
A king was born today
And man will live forever
Because of Christmas Day.

Joseph and his wife, Mary,
Came to Bethlehem that night,
They found no place to bear her child,
Not a single room in sight.

Hark now hear the angels sing,

A king was born today

And man will live forevermore

Because of Christmas Day

(After the choir's song. Everyone claps, and the pastor comes on stage.)

PASTOR:

What a wonderful night! What a glorious night! "And man will live forevermore because of Christmas day" Please give a clap offering to Jesus Christ. (Congregation claps.) Thank you! Hallelujah! Tonight, I will read from the book of Hebrews chapter 5 verse 8

(He reads)

"Son though he was, he learned obedience from what he suffered."

(Reads two times)

This is interesting. Jesus Christ, the Son of God, whom we celebrate today, came and learned obedience through suffering. Hallelujah! Who wouldn't think the Son of the Most High would come to the world to enjoy the best things in the world? No, God didn't plan it that way. He came to suffer, and what was the reward? Let's read further. Verse 9 says, (He reads.), "and, once made perfect, he became the source of eternal salvation for all who obey him. Praise the Lord!"

CONGREGATION:

Hallelujah!

PASTOR:

Jesus was born tonight to suffer for you and me. So what is it you are going through? Jesus suffered not because he sinned, but because he was destined to. And the Bible says that He learned obedience through the suffering. Maybe your suffering is for you to learn obedience. Swallow your pride and come to Jesus today. The choir sang just now, "that man will live for evermore because of Christmas day." If you would like to give your life to Jesus, I want you to stand up and come forward. Tonight is your night. (Dr. Thompson exchanges look with Mr. Greg. Mr. Greg motions for him to go forward and he does. He kneels in front of the pastor. Pastor prays for him.)

(BLACKOUT)

SCENE SIX

(Thompson in his apartment, he receives a call from Mr. Greg.)

DR. THOMPSON:
Hey, old man.

MR. GREG:
Hello, fella.

DR. THOMPSON:
Merry Christmas!

MR. GREG:
Merry Christmas! Significant decision you made yesterday.

DR. THOMPSON:
Thank you. And thank you for all time. I really appreciate you.

MR. GREG:
You're most welcome. I got a surprise phone call today. Can you guess who it was from?

DR. THOMPSON:
Social Security office.

MR. GREG:
What? Try again.

DR. THOMPSON:
Well, I don't know. Just tell me.

MR. GREG:
My wife called me this morning.

DR. THOMPSON:
Your wife?

MR. GREG:
She is visiting with my daughter tomorrow.

DR. THOMPSON:
Wonderful Jesus!

MR. GREG:
You can say that again, because she was in tears, asking for my forgiveness for shutting down on me for that long.

DR. THOMPSON:
So, what did you say?

MR. GREG:
Nothing.

DR. THOMPSON:
Nothing?

MR. GREG:
(In a funny way)
I said Aye, Aye, sir!

(They both laugh)

DR. THOMPSON:
You are so funny. I am thrilled for you. Your restoration is back in time.

MR. GREG:
That is the best Christmas gift I could ever ask for. Before I forget, the girls have a Christmas dinner tonight and they would like for you to be there. Can you make it?

DR. THOMPSON:
Yes, I will.

MR. GREG:
Hmm… I know you have an eye for that girl. She is a good girl, but do me a favor. Pray before you commit yourself to it.

DR. THOMPSON:
Aye, Aye, sir!

(They both laugh)

(BLACKOUT)

THE END

TRANSLATIONS

The song on page 9

Oni lojo ayo re, lojo ayo re — Today is your day of joy

Lojo ayo re/2x — Your day of joy

Iyawo abibeji b'Oluwa bafe/2x — The bride will have twins if God wishes

Eje ojo ooo eje ojo — Let her dance

Iyawo ojo latana, eje ojo — The bride has not danced since yesterday

Page 11 line 2

Ekule nbi o. Talo wanle oo? — Hello. Who is at home?

Page 11 line 10

Ekule oo! — Good day!

Page 13 line 7

Mi bimo ale ri, Oloun maje! — My child will never be a bastard!

Page 17 line 11

Oko miii, se alaafia lo wa — Hope you are in good health

Page 17 line 13

Beeni maami — That's true my mother

Page 18 line 24

O daaro. — Good night.

9 781735 367187